HeNRY HECKELBECK

and the Race Car Derby

By **Wanda Coven**

Illustrated by **Priscilla Burris**

LITTLE SIMON

New York   London   Toronto   Sydney   New Delhi

LITTLE SIMON
An imprint of Simon & Schuster Children's Publishing Division
1230 Avenue of the Americas, New York, New York 10020
First Little Simon hardcover edition January 2021
Copyright © 2021 by Simon & Schuster, Inc.
Also available in a Little Simon paperback edition.
All rights reserved, including the right of reproduction in whole or in part in any form. LITTLE SIMON is a registered trademark of Simon & Schuster, Inc., and associated colophon is a trademark of Simon & Schuster, Inc.
For information about special discounts for bulk purchases, please contact Simon & Schuster Special Sales at 1-866-506-1949 or business@simonandschuster.com. The Simon & Schuster Speakers Bureau can bring authors to your live event. For more information or to book an event contact the Simon & Schuster Speakers Bureau at 1-866-248-3049 or visit our website at www.simonspeakers.com.
Designed by Leslie Mechanic
Manufactured in the United States of America 1220 FFG
10 9 8 7 6 5 4 3 2 1
This book has been cataloged with the Library of Congress.
ISBN 978-1-5344-8631-7 (hc)
ISBN 978-1-5344-8630-0 (pbk)
ISBN 978-1-5344-8632-4 (eBook)

CONTENTS

Chapter 1

GO FLY A KITE

Henry Heckelbeck and his best friend, Dudley Day, raced into the backyard.

Both boys stared at the tops of the trees. They watched the leaves flutter in the wind.

"This is a PERFECT kite day,"
Henry declared.

"Finally!" agreed Dudley.
The boys had been waiting for
a windy day for weeks.

Henry had a green-purple-and-blue kite. Dudley had a big rainbow-colored kite that was shaped like a diamond.

They grabbed their kites, invited Henry's dad, and then went to the park.

At the park, the boys passed a kickball game, picnickers, and a dad playing catch with his daughter. Soon they found an open area.

The boys backed away from each other so their lines wouldn't get tangled. Then they grabbed their kites in one hand and their spools in the other.

"Ready?" yelled Dudley.

Henry nodded. Then both boys began to run. They let out their lines slowly. The kites began to climb into the air. The more line they let out, the higher the kites climbed.

"Let's do some tricks!" Henry cried. He made his kite dive and spin. Dudley made his kite go in a figure eight. Then a huge gust of wind snapped Henry's line, and his kite flew away.

"Oh no! My kite!" Henry
raced after his runaway kite.

Dudley spooled his line and ran after Henry. Soon the wind began to let up, and Henry's kite began to fall.

Wisp! Wisp! Wisp! The kite swished toward the ground, and . . . *CRASH!*

Chapter 2

THE STARTING LINE

The kite crash-landed on top of Sugar Hill.

The boys charged after it. Then Henry fell to his knees and grabbed his kite. Dudley plunked down beside him.

"How does it look?" asked
Dudley.

Henry flipped his kite front
to back. "It looks okay, except
for the broken line."

The boys flopped onto their backs to catch their breath from running so fast. That's when Henry noticed a huge inflatable arch at the top of the hill.

"What's that for?" he asked.

Dudley rolled onto his side and looked at the red arch. Across the top, in blue letters, it said BREWSTER'S FIRST ANNUAL RACE CAR DERBY.

"It's a starting gate for some kind of race," Dudley said. Beside the arch stood a tent with a line of people.

"Let's find out MORE," Henry said as he got up with his kite.

The boys hopped in line and waved for Henry's dad to join them.

"Wow, a Race Car Derby!" cheered Dad.

"What is a Race Car Derby?" asked Henry.

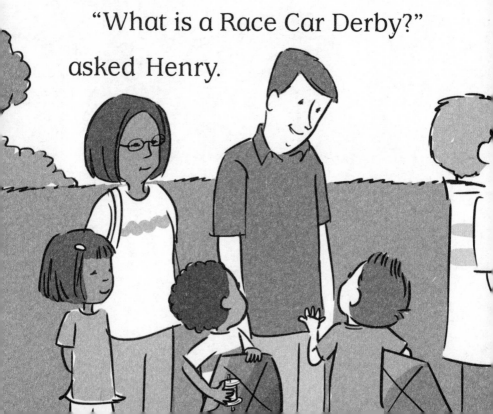

Before Dad could answer, a man in an orange cap handed them a flyer with a funky little race car on it.

"A Race Car Derby is a homemade car race," the man said, "only the cars don't have motors."

Henry and Dudley both raised their eyebrows.

"The homemade cars are raced on a hill, like this one," the man went on. "But in our race, the fastest car is not the winner. The car with the best design wins."

"Cool!" Henry and Dudley said at the same time.

Then the man in the orange cap asked, "Would you like to enter?"

The boys nodded wildly.

"When is it?" asked Henry.

"And how do we sign up?"
Dudley wanted to know.

"Everything you need to know is on the flyer," the man said. "We'll be selling car kits next week, and then we'll have the race on the first of the month."

Dad nodded and said, "This sounds great. Maybe Henry and Dudley could help spread the word?"

"Sure! Take more flyers for your friends," the man said. "The more racers, the better!"

Chapter 3

FAST FLYERS!

On Monday, Henry and Dudley brought the flyers to the cafeteria.

Max Maplethorpe slid her tray onto the table and sat down.

"What are those for?" she asked.

Henry handed a flyer to Max. "Brewster's having a Race Car Derby!"

"COOL!" she cried.

This got the attention of her cousin Melanie at the next table. Melanie raced over and said, "Can I see?"

Max hid the flyer behind her back. "Get your own!"

Melanie fixed her eyes on the boys and snatched a flyer from Dudley.

"Thanks so much," she said with a fake smile on her face. Then she yelled to her friends, "You HAVE to see this!"

Stanley Stonewrecker looked at the flyer.

"Wow, I've always wanted to be in a Race Car Derby!" he exclaimed.

Kids from every grade started taking flyers from Henry and Dudley's table. When they were about to run out, some kids began to argue.

A sharp whistle pierced
the room. It was Principal
Pennypacker.

"What is going ON?" the principal asked.

Henry stood up. "We brought flyers for Brewster's first-ever Race Car Derby, but there's not enough to go around."

BREWSTER'S
FIRST ANNUAL
RACE CAR DERBY

He handed his last flyer to
the principal.

The principal read it and said, "Well, this sounds like FUN! I can make more copies for the students!"

Everyone cheered except Henry. He had begun to worry. *If everyone enters the Derby, then how will MY car stand out?*

Chapter 4

CAR KITS

On Saturday morning, the Heckelbecks headed for the park with a picnic.

Henry brought his red wagon. They had to wait in a long line.

"TWO entry forms, please!" said Henry when it was their turn.

"Hey, I remember you!" It was the man in the orange cap.

He handed the forms to Heidi and Henry.

"The race is in a few weeks, so you'll have time to build your cars," the man said. "It starts at nine, but arrive an hour early. All cars have to be inspected for safety."

The Heckelbecks went to the next tent to buy car kits with special wheels.

"What makes the wheels special?" Henry asked.

A worker pointed to the edge of each wheel. "See these little nubs? They help the grass."

Henry looked closely at the nubs on the wheels. "Wow, so these wheels are actually good for the grass!"

"When your cars roll over the park grass, the nubs leave little holes in the ground," she explained. "Those holes allow air, water, and food into the soil to help the park grow!"

Henry thought that was
cool. He also thought the kit
was heavy! Luckily, the worker
helped him load the kits onto
Henry's wagon.

Once everything was in place, the family made a pit stop for a picnic lunch.

"Would anyone like help designing their cars?" asked Dad.

Henry frowned. "Nah, I want to think up something all by myself."

Dad turned to Heidi.

"Thanks, Dad," said Heidi,
"but Mom already said she'd
help me."

Dad shrugged. "Well, I'm always here if anyone needs me! But right now I need this sandwich."

Henry agreed, and everyone chowed down.

Chapter 5

THE MAGIC ANSWER

Henry sat down at the kitchen table with a pad of paper and a pencil. He thought about what kind of car to make. First he drew a soccer ball on wheels.

Nah, he thought as he crossed it out. *I always do soccer.*

He doodled a picture of his school desk on wheels.

Wouldn't it be funny to race down the hill sitting at my desk? he thought. *But who wants to think about school on a SATURDAY?!*

Henry went to his room
to search for more ideas. He
studied his toys and books,
but nothing was right.

Then he noticed that old weird book lying on his bed. It had that eerie glow.

The book rose from the bed
and floated across the room.
It landed on Henry's lap. *Pip!*

Henry instantly knew exactly who he wanted to help him.

He set the medallion down, and a shower of sparkles swirled around his room.

The medallion popped off the cover, and the chain came to rest around his neck. The book opened to a spell.

The Magic of Asking for Help

Are you having trouble coming up with an idea for a special project? Does it feel like all your ideas are boring with a capital B? Well, worry no more! If you're looking for a good idea, then this is the spell for YOU!

Ingredients:
1 friend or family member

Put your medallion down for this spell. The only magic you need is from your friend or family member. Find someone you trust and ask them for help. But if you like magical chanting, you could try:

Magic _____
Name of friend or family member

with ideas so grand,

lend me now a helping hand.

All his toys and the books
he had looked through were
put neatly back in place.

Then Henry went to find his
dad.

Chapter 6

A CAR IS BORN

Henry found Dad at his workbench in the basement. Dad lifted his safety goggles and rested them on his head.

"Hi, buddy," Dad said. "What's up?"

Henry smiled. "Will you help me think of an idea for my race car?"

Dad rubbed his hands together and pulled another stool out.

"I thought you'd never ask!" he said. "Let's brainstorm! Have you considered a tree fort car?"

Henry hopped onto the stool. "Well, I love tree forts, but we just built one. Can we try something new?"

Dad swiveled side to side on his stool. "How about a rubber band car?"

Henry shook his head. "Too rubbery."

"Maybe a dragon car?" Dad suggested.

Henry hopped onto the stool. "Well, I love tree forts, but we just built one. Can we try something new?"

"I thought you'd never ask!" he said. "Let's brainstorm! Have you considered a tree fort car?"

Henry smiled. "Will you help me think of an idea for my race car?"

Dad rubbed his hands together and pulled another stool out.

Chapter 6

A CAR IS BORN

Henry found Dad at his workbench in the basement. Dad lifted his safety goggles and rested them on his head.

"Hi, buddy," Dad said. "What's up?"

All his toys and the books he had looked through were put neatly back in place.

Then Henry went to find his dad.

Put your medallion down for this spell. The only magic you need is from your friend or family member. Find someone you trust and ask them for help. But if you like magical chanting, you could try:

Magic _____
Name of friend or family member

with ideas so grand,

lend me now a helping hand.

Henry instantly knew exactly who he wanted to help him.

He set the medallion down, and a shower of sparkles swirled around his room.

The medallion popped off the cover, and the chain came to rest around his neck. The book opened to a spell.

The Magic of Asking for Help

Are you having trouble coming up with an idea for a special project? Does it feel like all your ideas are boring with a capital B? Well, worry no more! If you're looking for a good idea, then this is the spell for YOU!

Ingredients:
1 friend or family member

"No dragons," Henry said quickly. He hadn't forgotten about when his toy dragon had come to life. What a disaster!

Dad rubbed his chin. "How about a snail car?"

Henry made a scrunchy face. "Really, Dad?"

Dad laughed. Then he got up and went to his private soda refrigerator. He worked for a soda company called The FIZZ.

"Maybe this Go Go Grape soda will kick-start our ideas," said Dad.

"YEAH!" Henry said.

Dad handed a soda to Henry and asked, "What kind of car do you want?"

"I'd like a car that says something about ME and my life," said Henry.

Then he took a sip of soda. The bubbles tingled and tasted like fizzy grape lollipops.

He drank some more, and
suddenly his eyes lit up.

"I've got it!" Henry cried.
"And it's a fizz-wizzer of an
idea!"

Chapter 7

SECRET CARS

When Henry had finished drawing his design, it was time to build his car!

He went straight to the garage, but there was a big problem waiting for him.

And the big problem's name was Heidi.

"Hey!" yelled Henry. "You can't use the garage. I called it."

Heidi huffed loudly. "Well, I called it first!"

They faced each other in an epic brother-versus-sister staredown.

"Kids! You can both work in the garage," said Dad.

Then he hung blankets across the room like a wall.

"Heidi, this will be your very own private building area," Dad said, pointing to the left.

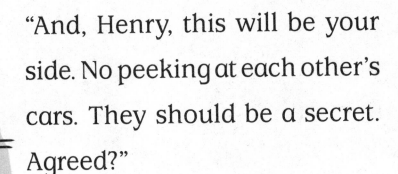

"And, Henry, this will be your side. No peeking at each other's cars. They should be a secret. Agreed?"

Everybody nodded. Then both teams got to work.

First Henry and Dad built
the car frames and attached
the wheels to the axles. They
also put together the brakes
and the steering wheel.

Dad showed Henry how to
use a power drill. They used
it to attach the seat.

Next they worked on the body of the car. Every kit included the same pieces of wood to make a racer, but Henry wanted his to stand out. He pulled out his drawing and studied it with Dad.

"Okay, I know what to do," said Dad. He used a saw to cut the wood into smaller strips. The strips could bend.

Then Henry and his dad started shaping the body. The car was round with a thick front and a skinny back.

When they finished, Dad asked, "Well, Henry, does it look like what you pictured?"

"Nope," said Henry. "It looks even better!"

He ran over and hugged his dad.

"Great!" said Dad. "Now all that's left is to paint it!"

Henry smiled a sneaky grin and rubbed his hands together.

Then he whispered so Heidi couldn't hear him, "Actually, Dad, the race car needs one more secret part."

Chapter 8

AMAZING RACE!

Henry and Heidi kept their finished cars hidden under blankets all week.

On race day Henry and Dad took their car to the inspector's booth.

The inspector tested the frame, the wheels, the steering wheel, and the brakes.

"This is quite a car!" the inspector said as he stuck a sticker of approval on Henry's seat.

Then Henry and Dad hid the car under a blanket again before rolling it to the waiting area with the other racers. The crowd began to pour in.

Each race put three cars against one another. Henry listened as the announcer called out the first three names.

"Would Heidi Heckelbeck, Lucy Lancaster, and Bruce Bickerson, please get ready to race?"

The drivers rolled their cars to the starting line, climbed in, and strapped on their helmets.

Bruce had a robot car. Lucy had a candy car. And Heidi had a magic car that looked so cool. Maybe too cool.

Did Heidi really use magic? Henry wondered.

"Ladies and gentlemen!" cried the announcer into her megaphone. "Are you ready for Brewster's very first Race Car Derby?"

The crowd cheered.

"Okay, drivers!" she said.
"On your mark! Get set! Show
off your car!"

The cars rolled down the starting ramp and bumped down the grassy hill. Bruce's robot car had floppy arms that waved wildly as he drove. Plus, it talked! It said the same thing over and over: "I am the Bruce Bick-a-Noid. I am a WINNING car."

Lucy's car was covered with candy. Plus, she threw yummy treats to the crowd.

Heidi's car sparkled with glitter. The sides had magical trinkets attached, like a genie's lamp, a unicorn, a crystal ball, feathers, and a wand.

Everyone clapped as the cars crossed the finish line. Henry was no longer worried about Heidi's car, because it wasn't really magic. It only looked magic.

Phew, Henry thought.

But then the announcer called out Henry's name, and he started to worry again.

Chapter 9

THE BIG REVEAL

Henry carefully rolled his covered car to the starting line and could not believe what he saw. He was racing against his two best friends, Dudley and Max!

Dudley's car was shaped like a kite.

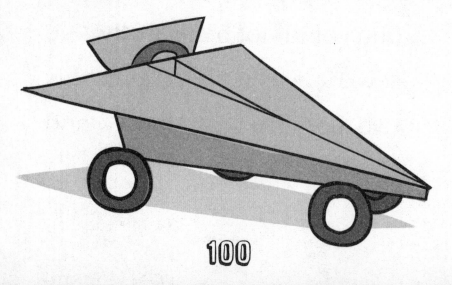

Max's car looked like a paper airplane.

Now it was time for Henry to show off his car. He whipped off the blanket, and everyone gasped.

Henry's car was shaped like a giant soda bottle. He called it The Soda Machine. The neck of the soda bottle was at the

back of the car. The seat was in the middle, and hidden inside the car was a secret bubble machine.

Each kid climbed into a car and strapped on their helmets.

"Okay, drivers!" said the announcer. "On your mark! Get set! Show off your car!"

Suddenly Henry was rolling downhill, and the crowd cheered.

Dudley had four smaller kites attached. And Max looked like a real fighter pilot in a real paper airplane!

Now it was time to pop open his super secret. Henry flipped a switch, and sparkly soda bubbles exploded from his bottle top!

The crowd went wild!

Max crossed the finish line
first, followed by Dudley.

Henry finished last, but he
couldn't stop smiling.

Chapter 10

THAT'S SODA COOL!

After the race, drivers showed off their cars and answered questions. A group swarmed around Henry.

"How did you make bubbles?" asked a girl with short hair.

Henry pointed to the middle of the bottle.

"I put a bubble machine INSIDE my car," he explained. "It keeps bubbling until it runs out of bubble stuff."

A man with a beard raised his hand. "How did you think of a soda bottle car?"

Henry smiled proudly. "I got the idea from my dad. He invents sodas for his company, The FIZZ. His job is really cool, and when I grow up, I want to be like him."

Then the announcer stood on the stage. It was time to announce the winning cars.

"Good morning, Brewster!" she began. "Thanks for making our first annual Race Car Derby a huge success."

The crowd clapped and cheered.

"And now to announce our winners!" she said. "In third place we have Heidi Heckelbeck's magic car!"

Heidi skipped onto the stage and was given a gift card for ice cream.

The announcer quieted the crowd. "In second place we have Bruce Bickerson and his robot car!"

Bruce acted like a robot as he walked onto the stage. He got a gift card too.

"And in first place," the announcer said with a long pause, "Henry Heckelbeck and his soda pop car!"

The crowd roared for Henry.

He jogged onto the stage and shook the announcer's hand. She gave him a golden trophy with a race car on top.

Henry held it as he ran straight to his dad.

"I couldn't have done this without you," he said.

Dad wrapped his arms around his son.

Heidi came over and said, "Hey, you two. Guess what goes great with soda? Ice cream!"

Henry laughed. "That sounds SODA cool to me."

Check out the next book starring

HENRY HECKELBECK

Clump!

Clomp!

Clump!

Henry opened and closed the cabinet doors in the family room.

An excerpt from *Henry Heckelbeck Dinosaur Hunter*

"What are you looking for?" asked Mom.

Henry said, "I'm looking for my FAVORITE shovel."

Mom raised an eyebrow. Henry had a lot of favorite things. He had a favorite magnifying glass. He had a favorite soccer ball. He even had favorite pirate coins. But Mom had never heard of a favorite shovel.

An excerpt from *Henry Heckelbeck Dinosaur Hunter*

Henry's older sister, Heidi, hadn't heard of it either.

"You have a FAVORITE shovel?" she asked with a huff.

Henry sighed. "Well, of course I do! Doesn't EVERY kid have a favorite shovel?"

Heidi snorted. "I definitely DO NOT have a favorite shovel. And why do you need a shovel, anyway?"

An excerpt from *Henry Heckelbeck Dinosaur Hunter*